By Malcolm A. Ivy

ANYTHING

"Does the quietest actions of pure people, always fall victim to proximity of the deafening actions of the wicked ?"

For Stephanie

ANYTHING

CHAPTER 1

SUMMER PLANS

Almost turquoise but not quite teal, I could stare at that lake for hours. The water was not sarcastically blue, in fact it had some character to it. It moved mechanically from left to right, almost synchronized with the clouds above it. The flowers perfectly in bloom swayed in the wind. I saw my wife in clean white linen enjoying the picnic and I saw my infant daughter lounging on the quilted pallet in the field. I could tell by their faces that we were enjoying our time together. I could tell by the dimples on my wife's cheeks, and I could tell by the glee on my daughter's face casting shadows of hope and excitement on her gleaming brunette curls. Sadly, I would toss away this vision based on the lie that it is, knowing full well of my daughter's blonde curls.

Like that, they vanished from the room, as a puff of smoke would from an extinguished candle, lingering around the wick and dissipating into memory. My world filled with the sounds of pans and pots clinking in the kitchen downstairs as well as the frustrated screams of a little lady who owned those golden curls. I looked out the window to see a fine August day. The birds were singing and the sky was calm. I glanced at my nightstand where I saw a photo of my wife Sam, and our daughter playing in the sand at the beach. It was one of my favorite photos. Every time I saw it, it only filled my heart with joy. I swiveled out of bed, to place my feet into my slippers and with some hesitation, I rocked forward in order to gain both momentum and the energy to stand up.

I grabbed my housecoat and wrapped a small bow to my side as I decided to venture downstairs for breakfast. Descending from our bedroom, the sounds became clearer and the sights more vibrant. Where I could see my wife multitasking in front of our stove, and at the same time entertaining our small toddler with great success.

 "Good morning everyone, how are my two favorite ladies this morning?" I said out loud as I physically held back a yawn. Samantha paused for a moment and kissed me on the cheek in response to my good morning. My daughter was bouncing with joy as if she hadn't seen her father for quite some time. It's moments like these that make strange dreams worth dreaming.

There is no place I could imagine better than here, and no people rather to be with.

Out of my peripheral vision I saw that Sam had made a splendid summer breakfast for all of us.

Eggs, sausage, and pancakes. I noticed that the little one was fussy today because there wasn't any food for her. Sam informed me that the milk man was running late per usual. Her slight frustration trickled into the flipping of her pancakes. I eased her concern in knowing that he always arrived at the right moment. "I know that George, it would still be nice to have breakfast on time for once" she slightly smiled and leaned her head back into my arms in gentle relief. I didn't want the little guy to feel the full might of the Carter household, he was new on the job and he was probably talking with his friends, or a girl and lost track of time. We were all young once.

I'm sure there will come a day where my little Grace will fib to her daddy about where she was, and with who. Hopefully, that world would happen no time soon. We glanced at our daughter playing with her dry, milk-less cereal bowl.

I sat down in my spot at the table to see that at least the newspaper boy had his priorities in order. I began to look through the articles. I try to keep to the positives, and mostly the comics. Otherwise you end up in the most pessimistic journalism you've ever read.

Most page articles just sound like fear mongering these days. Like this one "Protect Yourself Against Your

Communist Neighbor", or this one
"Banks No Longer Money Safe",
or this one, "Crime Up, Safety Down."

Are any of these true? Sam loves to
read them. She can be a bit nosey
about things like that. I tend to let
sleeping dogs lay. I don't go looking
for details that often… unless it has
anything to do with my favorite radio
shows.

I tend to read the better sides of the
paper. For example "Clover wins 1943
Gallup Races". Things like that place a
smile on not just my face, but I'm sure
countless others as well.

We soon gave up on our dreams of
milk and decided to feed Grace
something different instead. Sam and I
were discussing some plans for the
long weekend as I started to scour the

newspaper for some upcoming events. I suggested having a nice long picnic, or a nice trip to the beach. She suggested a nice sailing afternoon on her father's dirty old boat. I thought that was a great idea, Grace has never been on a boat before and this would be a wonderful opportunity for her, and that we should give him a call today.

Right as we were in the middle of our breakfast talk, Sam informed me that her brother called earlier today. I knew that he wasn't her favorite person in the world and I knew that she only tolerated him based on their familial connections. She told me that he called specifically to speak with me. I was a bit in shock fully aware that him and I don't usually talk as much. It seemed very odd and out of character for him. I was very concerned by her news so I asked her if everything was alright. She said that he wouldn't tell her what the inquiry was about.

I became very curious about why he would want to speak to me specifically. There was no previous conversation that we could continue or talk about, and it must have been important enough to bypass his only sister entirely. I then asked Sam "Around what time did he call this morning?"

"Around 4:30 this morning I'd say." She replied as she rolled her eyes into the back of her head and sipped her morning tea.

"Well then!" I exclaimed, "I at least owe him a call."

I got up from the table while my family continued eating and dialed the number to James's house. Having James live a couple of blocks away, made it much stranger in my mind that if this message was this urgent, he would have physically came here. Regardless, my curiosity wanted a much quicker resolve than getting dressed and driving all the way to his house. The phone rang a couple of times until James frantically picked up the phone without the proper greeting and hello. "Hey George, did Samantha tell you to message me?"

I told him that she did and asked was everything alright? My concern was reaching a very high peak. He assured me that everything was just dandy, but wanted to know if I would be able to deliver a package for him. I thought it was peculiar, knowing that he has a car at his disposal, in fact, he has a better car than mine. I asked him out loud, so that Samantha could hear me, "You said you need me to help deliver a package for you today?" I glanced over at Sam to gauge her face. As the receiver dangled from my ear. She looked at me with wide eyes, and a don't you dare demeanor. As you can tell, my wife can get her point across without saying a word. I understood exactly what she meant, through her stare and pursed lips. Sadly my curiosity and non-confrontational personality blindfolded my logic, and I continued on with my conversation by asking "what time did you need me to pick it up, and which post office did you need me to deliver it to?"

In my peripheral I could see Sam's head fall in disbelief, as I quietly mouthed "I'm sorry" in her direction. James assured me that it wouldn't be any trouble, and that the package was at my house. In fact, it should be sitting on your stoop at this very moment. My brow shrunk a bit on my forehead, trying to understand why it would be at my house.

I asked "Is it for us? Should I open it?"

James almost beat me to the end of my question and said "No! It's a surprise…. for… Sam." He went on to say "Think nothing of it, and bring it here at your earliest convenience."

I told him, "Would after breakfast be ok?"

He said. "That would be perfect and be careful with the package it is extremely delicate." I then verbally confirmed with him that I would be right over after breakfast. I could see Sam's arms tossed in the air in silent frustration. We then concluded our conversation and I hung up the phone. From one unnecessary conversation to the next unavoidable one.

Sam asked "Why would you help him and jeopardize our long wonderful weekend?"

I informed her that I didn't see the harm in getting it out of the way early, that's why I would go right after breakfast and deliver the package so we never have to think about it again. Sam assured me that hopefully this is the last time we help him with these nonsensical, abrupt, half baked errands.

"What is it even for, and why can't he do it?" She asked. Both of those answers I couldn't tell her, the first one because I couldn't say, if it was to be a surprise, and the second because I have no idea. I went to go investigate the front of our house to see if there was indeed a package. I opened the door to see a pale brown box, with no postage stamp or twine. Just a brown paper box with a small note that read "For George." Next to the box, was our two pints of milk that seemed a bit warm now.

I grabbed all three items and brought them in. I couldn't bare to see Sam even more flustered, so I told her the milk was fresh, and I just saw him deliver it a few seconds ago. Her chipper demeanor returned from this slightly good news and she proceeded to put it in the refrigerator as I clutched the package behind my back in order to shroud it in mystery, as if it wasn't already. I ran upstairs, keeping the package on my side and out of sight. I placed the package in the bathroom as I showered, got dressed, and prepared for the day my family and I were about to have. I even selected the shirt Sam picked for me for Valentine's Day to lighten the mood.

All I could think about was what was in that package? Part of me wanted to open and reseal it, it would be easy to do. However, my honest character and personality wouldn't allow my curious hands to venture onwards.

As soon as I was ready for the day, I flew downstairs and into the garage, so I could take this mystery box to James's house. I told Sam that I would be leaving and getting some gas. I asked Sam to call her father about the boat while I was out. I almost threw the package into the back seat, but mid toss I remembered I had to be careful due to the delicate nature of the package.

As I was on my way to his house, I looked at the package in the rearview mirror and thought to myself, Sam is right, if this is supposed to be a surprise for Samantha, why would it be on our porch for us to deliver to his house? Better yet, why is my name on the package instead? None of this makes any sense, but who am I to judge, maybe there was a perfectly good reason for all of this. I started to drive down James's street, where I could see his house hidden behind the bushes and trees of the neighborhood. I started to pull into his driveway but couldn't. It seemed as if there were multiple cars in the way, cars I didn't recognize at all. They all looked very nice and new, and a little out of place for this middle class neighborhood, but who am I to count someone else's pennies, it is clearly none of my business.

Apparently my business involves delivering secret packages for secret reasons. I parked some houses down, and walked back toward his front door. I walked up his front steps firmly grasping the package. As I reached for the brass, art deco doorbell, located shoulder height on his front door, I pressed it and waited for the door to open. I repeatedly glanced at my watch to keep track of the time that I now understood I was wasting.

CHAPTER 2

BUST

After three ticks the orchestra of locks jiggled and performed its way down to the doorknob. With a small vacuum of air, the door flung inward. Answering the door was a person I have not recognized, nor have I met before. He was wearing all black with dirty shoes that were leaving marks on James's beige tiled floor. The man hesitated for a second as he looked me up and down until his eyes rested on the package. His rough exterior softened, and proceeded to open the door wider to let me in.

I kindly removed my hat and walked through the entranceway. When I entered the living room I saw a gaggle of unfamiliar faces, the only one I recognized was James sitting on the distant couch. As soon as the door closed behind me, everyone stopped their previous conversation and placed their attention on me. However I could tell it was not me that they were interested in, but this mysterious package. I lowered the package from waist high to below my belt, anticipating with great confidence that the eyes would also lower in the same fashion. The only one now solely looking at me was James, he got up from his seat to greet me. "George" He said, "I see you have the package. Any complications?" He started to reach for the package but stopped as he made eye contact with me. I assured him that everything was fine, everyone was still looking at me as if I still had some level of interest.

James was completely enamored and transfixed on the brown box. So much in fact that he asked me to open it. With visual confusion I looked at him and noticed the graveness of his face. I then swiveled to view the same expressions on the collective group. Everyone was on the exact same page as James. I tried to slice the thick tension by saying "We sure want to make sure that Sam likes this gift right?" Though it was followed by a half developed and shy chuckle, I was the only one laughing.

I was obviously out numbered by the rest of the crowd, and I doubt my pacifist tendencies would even allow an honorable one on one with any of these folks. I decided to ask for a letter opener to rip the package. James quickly responded by denouncing my request. He suggested that it might be best for you to use your hands. I couldn't take him seriously until I examined the small bead of sweat marathon itself from the part of his hair to the top of his cheek.

I thought to myself, why was everyone emotional towards this package? Without further thought on the matter, I placed my index finger in the seam of the fold and quickly drug my finger across its surface ripping the brown paper. A small circle started to gather around me and to my surprise, it was another cardboard box with a lid. With a gentle motion, I slowly lifted the lid to find a beautiful, glass, necklace. I could tell it was glass based on the size of the diamond like gemstones. Otherwise James would have to had spent a small fortune that was unbeknownst to us. James was no longer making eye contact with me, but was staring at the silver, jewel encrusted necklace. A grin was starting to appear on his face, as well as everyone else. He moved in closer to examine it which I thought was peculiar, he looked as if he had never seen it before in his life, yet why did he pick it for Sam? His eyes bulged out of his sockets as if it was for him. I asked him what made him want to get this, and where did he get it?

He partially ignored me and said "It just looked so beautiful and like it could fix everything." I assumed he was talking about Sam and his relationship after their mother died, but I doubted that this was the tool to fix his absence and behavior. I started to notice that the time was getting late and Sam and I needed to get our day started. So I politely stated that it would be best for me to wrap this back up and head back home.

"I think we're going to the lake," I said "It'd be best for me to get a move on." I placed the necklace back into the box and started to turn toward the door where James grabbed my shoulder with more force than anticipated. Just enough force to be considered a catch and just shy of a grab. He stopped me from moving a single step further.

"Why don't you keep it here for me to clean it up and package it better? You can pick it up later tonight." I could tell he wasn't paying attention to me, due to him completely missing my remarks about the lake.

"I really need to be heading back, Sam and Grace are expecting me."

He looked at me with a quizzical look regarding the nature of Grace, "Who is Grace?" He said stirringly. Lividly I gazed at him informing him of his niece of two years.

"That's right" He said matter-of factly. "How is she doing? Is she doing well?" He asked in a mediocre, nonchalant kind of way.

My pettiness persuaded my behavior to resume by remarking "she's fine from the last time you saw her." I thought to myself that, that might have been a tad bit too harsh knowing that the last time James saw his niece was a year before her first birthday. James seemed to be concerned that I was fixing to leave with the package. He looked as if he was disappointed to be separated from his box. I asked him as I held the package close to my chest,

"Is this package not for Sam?" Just as he was about to speak, there was a brutish knock on the door. Everyone snapped their necks to the left to see who might be there.

The room grew silent and still, then another knock happened but this time more urgent. It seemed I was the only one curious on answering the door. I walked to the front door and slowly turned the lock. Before I twisted the doorknob, the door flung open and revealed the nature of our guests. It was a crowd of police officers, and agents who were now spilling into the already overpopulated living room. I was quickly brushed aside as the officers made their way into the house. It looked like a stream of blue and black hatted ants storming the unsuspected lunch. I noticed that there were enough policemen for each of

James's guests and then some. I could hardly believe what I was seeing, and it didn't seem real, it was like something out of a detective novel.

I looked in bewilderment as the scene unfolded before my eyes. Suddenly, a tall officer with a jet black mustache held an arm up across my chest both gently confining me to the corner of the entryway as well as securing the package in my possession.

"Wait, what is the problem officer?" I started to say as I scanned the room, guest after guest was grabbed from the furniture and held to the wall as I now was. There was no where to go, and nothing to do. I imagined that something very big might have happened, while I was in the center of this commotion it was hard to keep steady. There were enough officers here to make sure no one left. Whoever or whatever these officers were after, heaven help that poor soul. When I finally wrapped my head around the situation, a short man with bright red hair entered the room in business attire. He was in a plain white collared shirt, slacks, worn down dress shoes and a golden badge displayed on his belt. He removed his sun glasses and walked quickly to the middle of the room.

"Everyone remain silent, I'm only going to go over this once and I'll keep it short and sweet. You are all under arrest and will be processed shortly, boys, round them up and take them out to the wagon," He said gruffly. "You are all suspects in the theft. Late last night a priceless artifact was taken. Some key eye witnesses recognized some unfamiliar cars that were parked outside during the heist. The cars in questions are now coincidently, and some of you might say miraculously all parked in front of this house. So would anyone like to come clean before we get started?" A short moment of anxious silence filled the space as people were turned around and steel cuffs were placed on each of them.

I glanced over to make eye contact with James. Taking a page out of my wife's book, I made a face that accurately pleaded James to tell me what was happening. In full view of my attempts he completely ignored me. He looked to the detective and turned away, not making eye contact as he was whisked out the door past me. Unfortunately, I was terrified, I didn't have time for this, and I wouldn't spend a beautiful day set aside for my family being interrogated for a crime I didn't commit, especially if it was for James.

"Excuse me detective, might I have a word?" I said with the calmest voice possible. Before I could get the detective's full attention the tall officer holding me further wrenched the box out of my hands, turned me around and pressed me into the wall as he tightened the unforgivingly cold steel handcuffs on my wrists.

I heard the box being passed to another officer, the shuffling of cardboard, followed by an audible gasp. "Boss, we got it!" He exclaimed. Upon hearing his celebration I winced. Now whether I liked it or not, my name was involved in this investigation. I clenched my teeth as the detective moved to the right side of me so that even with my face pressed against the wall, I could make eye contact with him.

"Did you want something?" He said with slight amusement in his voice. "You now have my full attention."

"This is a giant misunderstanding," I gasped, "You see that package was dropped on my doorstep this morning, I don't know by who or for what, but my brother-in-law, one of the men you just hauled away, said it was a surprise for my wife and I should bring it over. I don't know who all these men are, or why they're here, but I am innocent. I was just returning a package that James had sent to our house on accident. Please, you have to believe me! My wife is waiting for me to come home."

The detective let out a heavy sigh and started talking in a slow monotoned voice, as if rehearsed. "Sir, so you have me to believe that a box…that was a gift for your wife… was dropped on your doorstep… and you drove yourself all the way over here to…give it to her…? Yes your correct, I'm sure it is a huge misunderstanding and this can all be discussed at the precinct. In the meantime, you have the right to remain silent."

"No, please, I don't know anything about this, and my wife is waiting for me to come home. Please at least let me call her so she isn't waiting for me!" I begged.

"Yea you'll get your call eventually,"He said, as dry as possible. Letting me know that any further conversations won't be happening. I was pulled away from the wall and drug out of the house.

I was forced to start my long march onto the stoop and out of the house toward the car. The yard was filled James's guests and the atmosphere was filled with the sounds of rights being read to men who are most likely guilty, but seem unbothered by the events taking place. I could also see a line of tow trucks centering the street, ready to dispose of what I assumed to be getaway cars and unregistered vehicles. I could see the line of individuals loading into the wagon going God knows where, and for God knows what. There was no possible way for me to travel in one of those things, because they were starting to fill up. So, I, ironically, was the only one to be shoved into the back of a police car. The officer lowered my head into the back of the vehicle and shut the door in my face as I was turning to ask a question of clarification. Shortly after, they strapped me in, both officers went in the front to drive away. I tried to communicate through the iron mesh separating us, "Officer there is a huge misunderstanding, I was merely dropping off a package for my wife, I don't even know these people." The one in the passenger seat looked at me in the rearview mirror suggesting I wasn't even worth the turn of his head.

"Is there anyway in which I can get some understanding around here?" I asked nervously, "I'm not sure why I'm in this predicament."

The one on the left looked to his partner and decided that minimal effort was needed to respond to me, in the form of not answering my question at all. I understood that not only was I alone in this situation, but I was ridiculously hopeless. My mind began to wander and circle around my family, all I could think of was Sam and Grace. How can someone like me get caught up in this mess? It seemed like some big joke.

Maybe Sam was in on this and she's waiting on the other side of where I'm going. Or maybe it's a surprise for my birthday, though it's not for another four months. Clearly, it's not real. I thought to myself whatever the issue was, if it was bad, it would be sorted out quickly. Innocent men do not pay for the actions of terrible men, and I am a good man, at least I'd like to believe so. Besides, that's why we have infrastructure and systems for things like this. If there ever was a mistake, in this case it must have been an honest one. The car ride lasted shorter than I anticipated, and I found myself outside of the police station. The car jolted to an abrupt halt and the officers retrieved me from the back. I exited the vehicle with the confidence I previously did not possess. As I walked up the ramp to the waiting area, an odd thought ran across my mind.

This isn't a big town, I would know because I have lived here my entire life, but what strikes me as odd is that we were the last to leave James's house, but we were the first car at the station. I thought that maybe they would have gone to a different building, yet my thoughts lingered on the question 'why would they'? The two officers held both of my arms as our foot steps echoed through the bleached, white, cinderblock walls of the jail. I could tell that I was their last bit of business for the day, and there would be no reasonings that could be had. The only words out of their mouths were sharp and sudden instructions toward me. They walked me into a room, occupied by two distinct gentlemen that were separated by wide open space. There was only one chair in the room that neither were sitting in. It sat in the corner lonely and unacknowledged. I was not going to be the one to state the obvious of our predicament. The officers unshackled me as I was then released into the room. The door clanked behind me as I turned to face the two strangers standing there. I really needed to call my wife, I was still mentally expecting her to pop out of somewhere, to surprise me with this joke that I have yet to find funny.

CHAPTER 3

SIGN

"Get comfortable, you might be here for awhile." The man in the cardigan said, "Grab that seat and make yourself right at home."

I slowly walked over to the right corner of the room where the chair sat bypassing the two men. I lifted the metal stool and carried it to the center of the room intelligently keeping my distance from the other gentlemen. I mentally sized them up based on their appearance and demeanor. The one on the right was an elderly man, much older than me, while the other seemed to be similar in age but less involved in his environment.

"Don't pay him any mind, he hasn't said anything since he got here." The elderly gentleman said in a flat tone. I quietly responded by nodding my head and showing my teeth.

I politely asked, "How long have you all been here?"

The man in the cardigan energetically replied with what looked like joy in his eyes. "Him, he's been here for about four days, I've been here for thirteen." My heart plummeted toward my lungs as I realized the depth of my troubles. I desperately needed to get out of here. I leaned a tad bit closer and asked if they had ever met Sam, my wife before. I looked at the other gentleman in the room only to see him react the same way he always has, by silently saying nothing. The other gentleman looked puzzled as if I was plucking obscure names out of the sky.

"Well, if Sam happens to be a lovely brunette nurse that gives us pudding on Fridays then yeah I've seen her on occasion. If not, then I apologize I haven't seen her nor do I know anything about her. All I know is that for a fella that looks and dresses like you, you sure like to ask a lot of questions."

The man smiled a bit, but only enough to see one sliver of his brass tooth peak beneath his upper lip. I stepped back from the man and proceeded to my assumed corner of the room. Now I began to take it all in, and absorb every piece of it. Every ounce of time I spent in that room I did so contemplating my entire life. I started to think of all the things that I used to take for granted. I thought of all the time wasted, and all the time I had given up for useless nonsensical things. Being in a room like this makes you think of your life in a new perspective. I never thought that at my age I would be contemplating the time I had left.

When have I ever thought I'd be in jail? I began to think of my parents and how they would view their child in a situation like this. Surely I'm speculating, but I have until this day never found myself in a more precarious position. All I could do is contemplate. I sat there staring at the walls as the lines from the corners disappeared from my vision until I was suddenly looking at a white void with three distinct characters in the foreground. Two of which were my cellmates and a chair that was sitting in the center of the portrait. For some odd reason I heard a small clink ring from beyond the cell. It almost sounded like a penny, or a small coin rattling on the hard floor.

Suddenly I could hear the synchronized steps of the police officer down the hall. The rubber of his soles faintly squeaked as it collided with the beige, yet dirty linoleum floor. The footsteps increased in volume by each motion forward until it reached a much anticipated halt. I could see through the crack of the door that someone had arrived, not only at their destination, but at their curiosity as to what is behind this door.

I could hear the jingling of keys dangling on their belt as the door graciously swung open to reveal a young man with listless eyes searching around the room. His eyes fluttered toward my direction and I could tell by his surprise that I was a face he was not accustomed to. He stared at me and then glanced downwards at the piece of paper, and then back at me once more. He repeated the number, followed by my name, still in shock he entered further into the room to solidify his request from me. This time he spoke louder and more clearly as if I had not heard him initially. I fumbled in my pocket to find the piece of paper they gave me on my way into the building. I finally flattened out the piece of paper from my pocket and looked through the details. At the top of the page I saw the corresponding number, I glanced back at the officer, confirming that I was the person he was looking for. He motioned for me to follow him as I'm sure he has rehearsed with others several times before. I emerged from my corner and followed him out of the room. On our way out, the man who has, for all of this time, sat quiet and motionless asked the officer a question. "Is there any good news today, Sir, if I could just write a letter to my daughter…"

The officer hastily replied, "for the umpteenth time, there are no calls to be made. Sit there… Sit still… and be quiet." To my surprise, and in such shock, I observed the man sitting in the room as he continued to do, all that I have known him to do. The officer closed the door behind me and we proceeded down the semi-lit hallway of the police station. I walked beside the officer, still in disbelief, but now in silence. I was internally wondering if I would ever get that chance to call my wife. However based on our previous encounter back there, I was unsure of how it would go. In my peripheral I glanced upward at the officer to gauge his demeanor, to see if he would be in any mood for questions. He paid no mind to me as we both charged forward down the hallway. He did not look at me, not even once, as it was his job to be steadfast and unwavering. Still, my wife and my child were worth every attempt at success.

So I asked him, "What did he do, the man back there, doesn't everyone get a phone call?" There was silence for a moment as the officer did not change his expression or gait. "Could I call my wife? There has been a misunderstanding. I promise my record does not have a single spot, let alone a stain."

The officer interrupted me by saying, "That man, back there, oh… he's the worst kind of people, an Arsonist." My eyes widened, both in disbelief of the officer acknowledging me and the news he shared.

"What did he burn?"

The officer sighed and softly replied, "Let's say class may be out of session for quite some time." My mouth gaped from the added context. I would have never thought of him doing that from our brief time together. The officer continued, "Some people don't deserve a call home. Let alone, a second chance."

"But sir, I am innocent. If anything I am guilty of a crime of proximity, that is all. I beg you, to let me call my wife. I know I am worth that chance and my family deserves that chance."

"Please stop talking." The officer said dryly. He thought for a moment and I could tell that there was something he was on the verge of saying while his eyes searched for reasons not to say it. I could tell that his heart wanted to lead him elsewhere, but he very seldom followed it until today. Looking at me sternly he said, "I believe you, people like you don't find themselves in here and I understand what it's like to be in the wrong place at the wrong time, follow me." My eyes swelled with emotion as I could see the compassion exude from his face. He diverged from our current path and went down a small hallway without breaking his stride.

I was speechless as I felt the tension release from my shoulders. I might still have a chance, I thought to myself. We stopped at a single black phone that was attached to the wall. The officer gestured for me to hold out my hand, as he fiddled in his pocket to present a single nickel. As I started to raise my arm, he placed the warm coin in my hand.

I picked up the receiver, and quietly deposited the coin. I felt the tension of the moment and wanted to hurry just in case the officer had an unfortunate second change of heart. I took a faint breath before calling the number then placed the receiver to my ear and waited. I could hear my heart beat through the hollow shell of the receiver.

As it continued to ring I looked up from the phone to see the officer facing away from me and looking back up the hall. He must be keeping watch for any other guards. I waited for what felt like an eternity, hoping and praying that my wife would be able to pick up. After a while I came to the conclusion that she's not picking up. I silently flagged the officer down, in order to not make a noise. I soon attracted his attention, and asked if I could have another coin. His face resembled that of an impatient yet understanding animal. He slowly turned around, and glanced back down the hallway.

"What do you mean?" He asked, "Give me a moment." He quickly walked up the hallway patting his pockets and looking around. When he reached the end of the hall, he turned around and doubled back with tremendous speed. He kneeled down and looked near the waste bin. He grunted as he pulled himself from the floor. "Quickly!" He eagerly stated. I nodded and deposited the coin, the spinning of the number dial felt like a slow death march. The ticking, and clicks of the dial became slower and slower on each number. I waited again, staring at the phone, my lifeline, and my last hope for saving myself, now seeming like an unimpressed observer, apathetic and uninterested.

I was waiting for someone, anyone to pickup, but no-one was. I glanced toward the officer who seemed very invested in the outcome of the call. I had to watch his compassion melt into apathy as his gaze hardened. Yet again no one answered. I looked back at him with my eyes begging for a 3rd chance. I thought to myself that I was lucky to get a first chance, let alone a second. But I was worth it, they were worth it. The officer discouraged, and bothered said "We have to go now, I'm sorry."

He grabbed me by the arm and he helped raise me up. I still held the receiver as I turned away. I had to let it go, as we made our way back down the narrow hall. I glanced back only briefly to see the receiver hang limply and swinging from its cord, as my hopes were deflated. "Where are we going?"
"I'm taking you to an interrogation room, you're going to have to give them a good story if you want to get out of here." He said flatly. "It's not likely, but I hope you get back to your family."

"How many people have you seen come through here like me?" I asked.

"I've seen many, but none like you."

"How many made it home?"

"None"

Frozen in disbelief, I wondered what might happen to me. The officer reverted back to his non-conversational personality. As we continued marching onward, I began to think about the other people at James's house, where are they? If they were truly guilty, why don't I see any of them here? It seemed quite odd that I was singled out for a crime that I couldn't have committed. Or maybe, this police station was for the innocent people. I swiftly discarded that thought knowing that in a room full of arsonists and similar individuals, I for sure was not in the good place.

We arrived at the pale door marked by the number 8. The officer turned to me in front of the frame of the door and asked me to place both arms in front of me. He reached on his belt and grabbed some handcuffs. I felt very betrayed and hopeless, but for some reason, I felt at peace knowing that all will be revealed when I explained myself. I have done nothing wrong so there is nothing to fear, and there isn't anything to change that. After each wrist was carefully shackled, I was led into the preoccupied room. There sat a woman in a white blazer and beside her, a gentleman wearing a grey tweed ensemble. They asked me to have a seat on the opposite side of the table. The woman went through her files without saying anything. The man hardly looked up from his notes as well, and I was sitting there waiting patiently, for my opportunity to clarify my situation. After a couple moments of silence I decided to interrupt their vigorous studying of the files, and as soon as I opened my mouth, she interrupted me.

"The artifact, what was it?" Her voice was as dry as sawdust, and her expression was nothing more than neutral.

"Excuse me?" I said. I couldn't understand why she would randomly bring up the necklace. She then went on to describe the details of the event.

"The necklace weighing 10.6 ounces, pear cut, yellow diamond, Egyptian opals, 13 karat pure white gold, know anything about it?"

I replied to her stating "No, I know nothing about it, but I have obviously seen it."

She still was not looking up from the papers, but was speaking to me in a condescending tone. However, in this one instance, her eyes did wander up in my direction and started to talk.

"You know nothing of it? With your fingerprints being the only fingerprints on the necklace I sure hope that you know something about it."

I saw out of the corner of my eye, the gentleman smirk under his breath as he tried to hide his mouth and maintain some form of decorum and professionalism. I was taken aback by how much they knew, and didn't believe. I needed them to understand that this was an entire mistake and a misunderstanding. I couldn't control myself, and I began to crack and ramble on hopelessly, panhandling for help on their part. I felt a lone tear exit my eye and I began to pour outward saying "Look here's what happened. I woke up this morning and my wife and I had plans. My brother-in-law called and said that there was a package outside that was for my wife Sam, and to bring it over to his house, where I opened it in front of all of those people. Then the cops broke down the door, took me here, placed me in handcuffs, and that is all that happened. I need to call my wife to see if she is ok, and to tell her that I am. They both looked at each other with some poorly hidden amusement and glanced back at me. The gentleman leaned forward and said, "Let me get this straight, you got a package… just delivered to your house… for your wife… is that correct?"

"Yes, yes, yes, that's exactly right!" I said with great enthusiasm.

He then went on to ask more questions. Saying "OK, then you drove that same package to your brother-in-law's house, where you opened it in front of all of these strangers, am I getting that right?"

My heart began to beat in a more normal tone, as I saw that they were starting to understand what I have been expressing this entire time. I even became more animated in my response saying, "Yeah, that's absolutely right! I didn't do anything wrong you see."

The gentleman nodded and physically affirmed his understanding. He then followed up by saying "Yes George, that makes so much sense, but I do have one question if you could help me clarify some small minor details."

I replied saying of course, and proceeded to listen to his inquiries.

He then sat back in his chair and asked, "If this gift was for your wife, Sam I think you said was her name, then why would you take it to James's house instead of giving it to your wife, who you said was home at the time?"

I was shocked to know that he clearly was not on my side, and required no explanation from me. Every word out of my mouth would simply validate their belief, and who would believe them? It sounds more than crazy. Hearing this logic from them out loud, confirms how illogical the truth was.

The lie was more logically sound than what actually happened. There was nothing I could say to convince them otherwise, and there was nothing more I could hope for. I started to politely beg both of them in the room. I banged my shackled wrists on the table, shouting "I did nothing wrong, I'm innocent, I didn't do anything wrong, I didn't do anything."

The woman stood up, and asked the gentleman to leave, as she had said she heard enough. The gentleman left the room, as did the guard who walked me in. Both men exited the room and only the two of us were left. She said "OK, based on the evidence of what we heard today, there are two outcomes, and only two. You have committed a felony of theft and had in your possession stolen property and property damage estimated between

6-13 million dollars. Which will result in a lengthy trial, most likely a guilty verdict and face federal jail time between forty-two and sixty-three years if lucky."

She reached into her files and pulled out a stack of papers for me to sign. She plopped them onto the table which caused a small thud. I was speechless, I could hear the ringing in my ears as I tried to comprehend my new reality. Logic left with the gentlemen from this room, and there I was greeting my new reality. My life once again flashed before my eyes, which felt like the very last time. I knew I would never call my wife again, I was sure I would never see my child again, for it has been decided regardless of my approval or understanding. I was staring at the book of information and the pen that sat beside it, I had no choice, I thought to myself. The chains jingled from my wrists as I reached for the pen. However, before I was able to make contact with the pen, she continued talking by providing a second option. She looked at me with a subtle smile and said, "Or… Rehabilitation could be the ticket for you."

She shuffled through her files and selected a bright blue folder and placed it next to the pen in front of me. She opened it and I saw a single sheet of paper and the only thing typed on the page was the line of text saying. "I agree to all terms and conditions, followed by an empty space for a signature. I asked her, "What is the Rehabilitation option? What are the terms and conditions? What does this option offer?"

She kindly addressed my questions with a statement, "You shouldn't see this as an option, but rather an opportunity."

I was throughly confused by this "opportunity" and asked her, "How long is the sentence?"

She stated as if rehearsed "The sentence is as long as you make it. It could be days, it could be weeks, but you would be free to go shortly after, and all charges would be dropped for this crime."

I sat there looking at both my option and opportunity, and I picked up my pen knowing that there's nothing I wouldn't do for my family.

CHAPTER 4

CLOUDLESS SKY

I signed my name with a sense of finality. The paper felt heavy under my pen, and the ink seemed to bleed into a future I couldn't see. The woman exited the room and knocked on the door three times as she left. Shortly after, two guards entered the room, rifles in hand. One of them was holding a blindfold and proceeded to place it on my head. As my worldview began to darken, I asked them if they were going to read me my rights. The only thing one of the officers said was, "you already covered that by signing."

The world around me vanished, replaced by an impenetrable darkness.

My only experience of this new world was through sound and the hands of the guards on each of my arms. I was led down the long hallway and through several doors very different from how I entered. Disoriented I entered a drafty room where every foot step echoed and the sound of an engine rang loudly in my ears, the smell of diesel told me that wherever I was going it would be a long journey. I was led up some stairs which led me to believe it was a bus. The guards guided me and pushed me down the narrow corridor of chairs that gently brushed past my hips. My shin hit the seat of the chair at the back of the bus. No longer feeling any guidance from the guards, I felt my way into the seat and sat down. As I was situated into my seat, the guards plopped into the seat next to me.

The silence on the bus was almost palpable. It felt as if I were the only soul aboard, the quiet stretching out into a void. I could feel the vibrations as the bus started its journey, moving away from the society and life I worked so hard to build. The familiar hum of suburban life faded, replaced by the unorganized bumps of the road.

Time passed slowly as the bus seemed to travel for hours, there was nothing for me to do, the only thoughts that filled my head were those of my family.

On both sides, I could feel the guards sitting next to me. The weight of their bodies pressing into the seats, and the butts of their rifles pressed against my sides. I tried to speak, to reach out to them, but my words were swallowed by the silence. They did not respond, nor did they move.

I sat there rocking back and forth from the bumps in the road, all the while imagining what awaited me, and how long I would be there. Surely, it wouldn't be for too long. After all, what do I have to rehabilitate? I'm innocent, I just need to be myself and I could go back to my life in no time.

I missed Sam, and I hope she was not too worried. I hate to think of how I've ruined our long weekend. I hope that they are both well. I just wish I had a way to let her know that I was OK, and I would be home soon. When I get back we will laugh, she may be a little mad, but in the end, we will laugh as we always had.

The bus came to a sudden stop. I heard the doors open, and the driver spoke, cutting through the silence. "Please remove your blindfold and make your way outside of the bus."

I hesitated for a moment, then lifted the blindfold from my eyes. The world came back into focus, and I yet again found myself in the dark. There were no windows on the bus, only small pinholes the size of a pencil bordered the top of each frame. I looked to my left, then right to see the guards still in their idle positions. They were looking forward without breaking concentration and I noticed they were catatonic and perfectly still, but unsettlingly still. Upon further investigation, I peered closer at their faces and to my surprise they were mannequins, fully dressed and fully equipped mannequins, sitting perfectly still beside me. It frightened me because for a moment, during the ride, I could have sworn I felt them breathing. Maybe it was the bumps in the road, or maybe it was just my imagination, I will never know.

I looked towards the front of the bus, expecting to see the driver. The driver's seat was empty, the keys still jingling in the ignition. The person who had driven the bus had vanished without a trace. I was looking around the bus to see who was speaking to me. I searched each bus seat and found nothing. A voice echoed from the front of the bus and seemed to come out of a radio speaker attached to the bus. "Quickly make your way towards the blue path." It said, directly after the doors of the bus opened.

I stood up and walked towards the front of the bus. I stepped down into a field of low grain, the stalks brushing against my legs as I moved. In the distance, I saw a facility. It looked like an empty garage, one of those new builds from the city, stark and industrial.

The building seemed almost skeletal, with hardly any walls or windows, just open space stacked upon open space. In the center of this structure was a tall pole, a beacon standing guard over the emptiness.

As I walked toward the building, I noticed a line of people. They were inmates, standing on both sides of the path in rows, dressed in black jumpsuits. Their faces were a mix of expressions, some blank, some curious, but all silent.

I walked down the path, feeling the weight of their gazes. The path was clean and well-maintained, a stark contrast to the rough road that had brought me here. The people were of varying sizes and shapes, a human corridor leading me forward.

At the end of this human corridor stood an individual in white. Her presence was striking against the sea of black. She smiled at me as I approached, her eyes sharp and assessing.

"Welcome," she said. "My name is Lisa. I will be giving you a tour of the rehabilitation center. Please withhold all of your questions until the end, as I know there will be plenty."

I nodded, my mind swirling with unspoken questions. The journey had only just begun, and already I felt the weight of the unknown pressing down on me. I followed Lisa, stepping into the future that awaited me behind the skeletal walls of the facility. The sky was perfectly blue with not a cloud in sight. I would enjoy it more in normal circumstances.

In the background, everyone began to disperse from their place in line and started to go about their business.

"Come this way, let me show you around the living quarters." Lisa said sweetly

The tour began with Lisa explaining the rehabilitation complex. "This place has three distinct areas," she said as we walked. The largest section was the living quarters, where food was provided four times a day: breakfast, brunch, lunch, dinner, and dessert.

She described the open-concept structure. "There are no walls here," she gestured around. "Just floors, pillars, and designated sections for everyone. There are privacy curtains for restrooms and showers, but beyond that, privacy isn't a practice here." The idea of living so openly made me visibly uneasy, but she seemed unfazed and continued the tour as if the statement was normal.

"You'll get really comfortable with your neighbors," she added with a smile. "At least, the good ones." Her words hinted at a mix of camaraderie and tension among the inmates.

We walked through vegetable and flower gardens, vibrant with life and color. There was also a recreational pool, its surface shimmering in the sunlight. On the side of the pool deck, was a bench just big enough for two people. Lisa invited me to sit, allowing me to finally ask my burning questions.

"How long have you been here?" I asked.

"Not long," she replied with a wry smile. "Long enough to learn my lesson. Time flies when you're having fun," she added sarcastically.

"And what about the other two areas?" I inquired, trying to grasp the full picture of this place.

"The test rooms," she explained. "That's where you get evaluated to see if you're ready to leave the facility. If you're cleared, all charges are dropped. If not, you stay."

I had noticed the absence of guards and asked why that was.

"We don't need guards," she said. "Control comes from the loudspeaker in the center of the compound. Every night, the speaker calls out inmate numbers. Those called go to the council buildings for evaluation. Some people come back, others don't. Eventually, everyone's number comes up. But you'll cross that bridge when you get there. Excuse me I will need to go prepare for dinner soon. I advise you to make some friends, get to know people, this is about to be a big journey for you. Maybe you'll learn something, not just about this place, but also yourself." She looked at her watch and got up to excuse herself from the conversation, but before she left I stopped her because that explanation seemed almost too simple.

"Why aren't there any guards at all?" I pressed. "What keeps people from just walking away?"

Lisa smiled, but her grin felt hollow. "Trust me, if you're concerned about people leaving, there's no exit. If you're concerned about people becoming unruly, the loudspeakers ensure order, and the evaluations keep everyone in check. You'll catch on quickly, soon enough."

I started to see everyone walk toward the main building as nightfall began, I started to follow the crowd into the building as I listened to the chirps of the hourly dings of the loudspeaker. They sounded like church bells without the reverberations. They happened every hour on the hour. I walked through the wallless corridors to the main cafeteria, we all funneled into the room, and I noticed that there were some that looked nervous, and some who didn't.

The door swung open as I approached the doorframe, and there I smelled the banquet.

Dinner that evening was an absolute feast. I sat at my designated section and struck up conversations with some of the other inmates. There was ham, turkey, quail, and duck. All this food, Lisa mentioned, was shipped in every morning along with other supplies. There was champagne and wine, making it feel like a celebration rather than a meal in a rehabilitation complex.

I glanced around to see if others were enjoying the feast as much as I was. Most seemed subdued, almost as if they were going through the motions. Some at my table were chatting, so I introduced myself. "Hi, I'm George," I said, looking around at the faces.

A man to my left smiled. "I'm Henry," he said. "What are you in for?"

I started to stammer out my answer when he decided to answer it first.

He chuckled. "I'm in for murder," he responded, as if discussing the weather.

I blinked, unsure how to respond. "Oh, um, okay," I stammered. "Anyone else want to share?"

The next man spoke up. "Jeffrey, arson."

"Alice, kidnapping," said a woman across from me.

"Alex," another man added tersely. "Harassment."

"Grace," a woman with a sharp look unlike my daughter said. "Theft—financial embezzlement from elderly centers."

Finally, a large man with an unsettling grin said, "Arnold. Conduct of war, decapitations, dismemberment... just for fun."

When they asked me what I had done, I said, "I'm innocent."

They all laughed. Jeffrey, through hysterical laughter, said, "Everybody's guilty of something. Even if they weren't guilty, they will be."

As they started to talk amongst themselves again I started to finish my meal, the taste of the food was unlike any other. I've never tasted anything quite like it, and the smells were something I would truly never forget. Some of the people who had the exact same dishes as myself seemed to not like the food and hardly touched it, almost as if they were eating it out of necessity rather than enjoyment. I then shifted back into reality, reminding myself that this wasn't any luxury resort, this was a place for terrible people who did terrible things, there is no enjoyment in this. Yet, for the life of me, if this was Hell's waiting room on earth, why was this the most tender cut of meat I ever tasted?

The loudspeaker interrupted, announcing the start of the night shift and instructed us to go to our quarters. We left in a single file line to our respective sections. I saw my bed for the first time, neatly made with cotton slippers on the side and satin sheets on the bed. A small piece of milk chocolate wrapped in gold foil and a glass of water adorned my nightstand.

We were instructed not to jump right into bed but to wait for the announcements. We stood to the left of our beds, waiting to hear our inmate numbers called for rehabilitation. Arnold, to my left, reassured me, "Don't worry. Your number won't be called. It's your first night. Everyone else is on the hook."

"Why should I be worried?" I asked, my anxiety creeping up.

Arnold smirked. "I'm sure we'll find out. Just try to relax."

A series of numbers I didn't recognize were called. One by one, those individuals walked in a line to the evaluation rooms, six at a time. Among them were Henry and Arnold.

Arnold said to me "This is my first. If I don't see you again, it was a pleasure meeting you."

They walked single file out of the room, and the rest of us went to bed. I noticed, however, that not everyone could sleep. The weight of the unknown hung heavy in the air. My mind raced with questions and doubts, wondering what fate awaited me in this strange, open place.

CHAPTER 5

SATIN

That night, I fell asleep with thoughts of my family swirling in my mind, their faces vivid yet distant. The ache of separation from them was a constant, gnawing presence in my chest. The room was filled with the soft rustle of others settling into their beds, the occasional murmur breaking the silence. Despite the overwhelming uncertainty and fear, exhaustion eventually claimed me, dragging me into a restless sleep.

I woke up abruptly, my face wet with tears, heart pounding in my chest. Nightmares had clawed their way into my sleep, filled with scenes of screaming, terror, and chaos. The sounds of my nightmares seemed to bleed into reality as I blinked my eyes open, trying to orient myself. The yelling and screaming were real, echoing through the compound, accompanied by the harsh clanging of tools and the slamming of metal doors.

I sat up, my breath quickening as I looked around in the dim light. A group of inmates stood by their beds, staring towards the evaluation buildings, their faces masks of fear and horror. Others remained in their beds, seemingly at peace, though I noticed some lay with their eyes wide open, unmoving, as if they couldn't hear the terrible noises at all.

The screams and noises gradually subsided, leaving an eerie silence in their wake. I watched as four of the building doors swung open while two remained shut, their silence ominous.

The loudspeaker crackled to life, instructing us to return to our beds or face acceleration. The threat was enough to send everyone scrambling back to their bunks, fear evident in their hurried movements.

I shuffled back to my bed slowly, my mind racing with questions and fear. As I moved, I saw two cars drive to the back of the buildings, then head towards the main road, their headlights cutting through the darkness. The compound doors creaked open, and I heard the footsteps of returning inmates. Their soft sobs filled the air.

Arnold's bed was near mine, and as he returned, I leaned over quietly and asked, "How did it go?"

He couldn't look at me. His face was ashen, eyes unfocused, and he seemed not to hear my question. He lay down mechanically, his body rigid, eyes staring blankly at the ceiling. He didn't blink, didn't move, as if he was in a state of deep shock. His reaction sent a chill down my spine. Whatever had happened during the evaluation had clearly shattered him, leaving him a shell of the person he had been earlier.

I lay back on my bed, the soft satin sheets and the neatly arranged cotton slippers beside the bed feeling absurdly luxurious in contrast to the turmoil within me. The small chocolate on my nightstand now melted, served as a surreal reminder of the odd comfort provided in this place of dread. I tried to close my eyes, but sleep escaped me, the night's events playing over and over in my mind.

I thought about my family, their faces now a source of both comfort and pain. I wondered how they were coping, if they missed me as much as I missed them. I thought about James, if someone as innocent as me was going through this much turmoil, I could imagine his situation.

The sobs of the returning inmates gradually died down, replaced by the soft hum of the night. I could hear the murmur and whimpering of the tyrants I once knew at dinner. As I lay there, I tried to piece together what this place was, what its true purpose might be. The open concept, the lack of guards, the bizarre evaluations—all of it seemed designed to strip away any sense of normalcy, to keep me perpetually off-balance.

My thoughts drifted back to Arnold. Whatever had happened to him was a warning of what awaited me, I'm innocent, I hope and pray they can see that. As the first light of dawn began to creep into the room, I realized that sleep would not come. I could only lie there waiting for whatever came next and hope for a different outcome than my peers.

CHAPTER 6

LEAP

The next morning, Arnold was physically present at breakfast, but mentally, he was somewhere else entirely. He had become somewhat of a celebrity overnight. People flocked to him, bombarding him with questions. "What happened? How did you fail your evaluation? Did the screams come from your room?"

Arnold didn't say a word. He just sat there, rocking back and forth, he didn't touch a single bite of food. His eyes were empty, and he seemed to be in another world. After a while, he stood up and walked back to his room, leaving behind a wave of whispers and speculations.

"They must have to fight each other," one inmate suggested, in a low voice.

"No, I think they have to go through some sort of test. Maybe they were tortured," another implied.

"I've heard they're evaluated by the thing they fear most," someone else added.

"Others believe they're brainwashed," replied another.

Whatever it is, it's terrible beyond belief. If those evaluations can make someone who enjoyed torture feel weak and powerless, then maybe it's the most unimaginable thing in the world.

Someone turned to me and asked, "What do you think happens in there? What's your biggest fear?"

I didn't hesitate. "Not seeing my family again," I replied. The mention of family opened the floodgates. Many inmates began talking about their loved ones, those who still had them. It was clear that the fear of never reuniting with family was a common thread that bound us all together.

Despite the conversation, I couldn't stop thinking about what was behind those doors. After lunch, curiosity got the better of me. While everyone was busy eating or wandering through the gardens, I decided to investigate.

I walked up to the evaluation rooms, my heart pounding in my chest. The doors were featureless, with no doorknobs or windows. They were just square rooms, wide enough to lie down twice in and a bit deeper than that. As I circled around the building, I found another door on the backside, this one with a keyhole that could be opened from the outside.

I leaned in closer to inspect it when the speaker crackled to life. "Please refrain from occupying this space and make your way back to the common areas."

Startled, I quickly ran back to the compound, where I ran into Alex from the night before. "What were you doing?" he asked, as he glared at me.

"I was just exploring," I replied, trying to sound nonchalant.

"Don't wander off too far, or you risk acceleration," he warned.

"Acceleration?" I asked. "I heard that term last night when everyone was looking out at the evaluation rooms."

"Acceleration means your number would be called quicker or multiple times," Alex explained.

"What happens if your number gets called multiple times?" I pressed.

"Well, apparently, the sessions get longer and more intense. Frankly, I've never seen someone survive acceleration. No one ever gets free after acceleration. It's very rare, but I'm sure it has happened. None that I've seen while I've been here."

"How long have you been here?" I asked.

"This is my third day," he answered.

"Your third day?" I echoed in disbelief. "I could've guessed at least this would be your third month. You look so skinny, like you haven't eaten in weeks."

"It's the food," he said, sighing. "The food is designed specifically for us based on your evaluations. Depending on how many evaluations you have, the quality of the food decreases. There's hardly any nutrition and hardly any taste, but it smells better than ever."

"That's impossible! The food was amazing, especially for a prison," I said.

He looked at me and said, "Yours was because you haven't been evaluated yet."

He didn't say anything more, and we both decided to get back to our sections. On our way back, he talked about how there have been people here who have been here for 10 days, 13 days, sometimes even longer.

I asked him honestly, "What do you think happens in those rooms?"

He paused for a moment, a tear beginning to fall down his face. I could tell he didn't want to talk about it, but he said, "What happens in that room is beyond the worst thing imaginable, and there's no one you can blame but yourself."

The loudspeaker interrupted us, asking us to quickly resume activities in the common area. Alex hastened his walk.

"Do you have children?" I asked.

"Yes, I do," he replied softly.

He told me their names and how he wanted nothing else in this world but to see them again. I told him that I had children too and how I really missed my wife. The whole thing happened so fast and unexpectedly.

He leaned in and said, "So you have to be honest. Did you actually do it? What did you do?"

"I am actually innocent, they seem to think that I stole a necklace." I explained.

"That's it? That's all?" he asked, incredulously.

"Yeah, and then they gave me the choice to go to jail or come here, so I signed up," I said.

He stopped, his eyes filled with anger and hurt. "Regardless of the time they were going to give you, you should've gone to prison. You didn't have a choice if you chose to be here. You were the dumbest person on this planet."

I paused and internalized what he just said, I now realized that this place was not for the faint of heart or weak spirited. As the afternoon wore on, I decided to talk to some of the people who had been here the longest. I explained to them that I didn't really understand how this was supposed to be a punishment.

One of them told me that they used to ship small animals for you to harm, others that they electrocuted you until you gave up secrets. Some thought this was just a place to put suspected communists. "As if they would give communists champagne and shrimp," someone scoffed.

But the scariest theory of all was that whatever you did in the outside world is exactly what they do to you in that room. A little relief washed over me, knowing I was completely innocent. Nothing should happen to me, but it frightened me that the people here had done things I couldn't even begin to imagine.

I worried about what if this place, or the people in charge, thought I did something worse. What if they decided to do something terrible to me? I had to find Lisa and get to the bottom of this before it was too late. I needed to call my family, this has gone on long enough.

As I looked at the dinner menu, to my surprise, it was a turkey feast. But I couldn't think about the food. All I could think about was how to clear my name and get out of this mess. I began to feel like I was going crazy. This place had so many wonderful things, yet I had no idea why I was here or what happened to people like me.

I started asking people around me if they had seen Lisa recently. I hadn't seen her since I got here. No one seemed to know the whereabouts of

Lisa, and if they did, they sure didn't seem to want to tell me. The closest thing I got to an answer when asking someone was, "I think she left, but she does come around often." I was filled with confusion as I replied,

"Left? Isn't she a prisoner like us, I mean… like you all?"

The woman studied me as she considered my remark and stated "knowing what she did, Lisa can do whatever she wants."

The woman quickly got up from her chair and strolled down the hallway, knowing that I would still be longing for answers.

I tried to distract myself with the books in the library until dinner arrived. At this point, it felt like a waiting game.

The table was set, and everything looked great. The food still smelled delicious, but everyone was quiet. I tried to make my way around the room to see if people could give me insight on what to expect.

I'd heard stories about people having to cut off their limbs, use power tools against innocent animals, and some even said people. No one really wanted to talk about their individual evaluations, Except for one.

Ryan Flask was quiet and didn't speak. He wrote down his story on a small napkin. "I could rip out the tongue in my mouth, but not the one in my wife's." He broke down in silent tears.

Seeing him like that made me very scared. I didn't know what to expect.

Then the loudspeaker turned on with an unscheduled announcement. Everyone froze after hearing the chimes of the loudspeaker. The bells rang earlier than expected. You could hear the forks and cutlery clink and fall to the table unanimously. The world stopped and anticipated what came next. Without introduction or prologue, the speaker began to call the names of five different people, however the last name was familiar and it was Arnold's. Arnold began to panic, he looked around in disbelief, spinning and clutching himself simultaneously. He became verbally unorganized and descended into madness. The people closest to him began to form a circle around him and distance themselves from his space.

His radius grew bigger as he tried grasping and pleading for someone to help. With no success, he darted out of the room and up the stairs, parting the sea of people in his mad dash towards escape. I ran after him to see what was going on.

I found him hiding in an upstairs room. He was trembling, his eyes wide with fear. "They wanted me to skin that animal," he said, his voice breaking. "I was blindfolded, and they said to skin that animal. I was going to until it started screaming. I heard a familiar voice. I couldn't... I couldn't! They're just going to get worse. Every time you don't do it, it compounds. It gets worse. I thought I heard my daughter in that room."

I asked him if his family was safe. He looked at me with despair. "Everything and anything can happen," he whispered.

For the first time since I arrived, I saw guards walking down the hallway. Arnold was so scared. He then jumped off the building.

No one but me was in shock. Shortly after, the loudspeaker announced my number.

CHAPTER 7

WHAT

I heard my name called over the loudspeaker, my heart pounding in my chest. The six members including myself assembled in the middle of the cafeteria. The five called before me were set to face their evaluations that night, and I was scheduled for the next morning. As we were herded toward our testing, the atmosphere grew tense and chaotic.

We all marched out of the compound and through the fields of grain toward the evaluation rooms. I watched as the five inmates in front of me were led to their individual evaluation rooms, their faces pale and eyes wide with fear. The guards were there to maintain order, some prisoners had to be physically forced into their rooms. The air was thick with desperation as prisoners screamed things like, "Please, not my family," "I can't do it," and "I'm not strong enough." One woman cried out, "This is not the price of freedom!"

The sight of their fear sent chills down my spine. I was informed that I would spend the night in my test room. We all got in line, preparing to be evaluated while everyone else in the cafeteria resumed eating as if nothing unusual was happening. One by one, the doors closed and locked behind us. I saw one man struggle and scream, needing to be dragged and tossed into his room.

When it was my turn, a guard escorted me to the last room. "Listen to all instructions," he said, then closed the door behind me. The room was empty except for a chair, a dangling light bulb, and a speaker on a side table. The bland, cold room only heightened my anxiety. I was informed that my test would begin separately from everyone else's and was asked to wait for further instructions.

As I sat there, the sounds from the other rooms seeped through the walls. I could hear the screams and cries of the other inmates. On the table next to me, there was a radio with a large black dial with five settings, each channel was labeled to a corresponding test room. It was currently set to the off position.

Curiosity and dread compelled me to turn the dial to channel one. I heard the familiar voice of the woman. I couldn't hear what was being said to her, but her responses were clear. She begged and pleaded for something different, anything else. "That's sick. I'm not going to do it. What type of life could I live afterwards?" she cried, followed by heart-wrenching weeping.

On channel two, the man who had been dragged into his room was begging for his freedom. His voice was filled with anguish as he cried about missing his family, unable to forgive himself, wondering what his mother would think and how he could ever look himself in the mirror again.

Channel three brought the sound of frantic hysteria. "How could I ever walk again? Please don't make me do this! You can't keep us here!" the person screamed.

One of the channels I heard said "That's it? That's what this whole this is about? Are you serious? This is so stupid."

The last channel filled with screaming, cackling, crying, and begging. Unable to bear it any longer, I turned the radio off and sat in the eerie silence. In that silence you couldn't hear a single thing. As if those rooms surrounding me and the people in them didn't exist. Thoughts raced through my mind. I wondered if I could go through with whatever they asked of me. The idea of causing such horrors for a chance at freedom was sickening.

I thought about my family. Could I endure pain for them? What if they wanted me to dip my hands into a vat of acid or cut off my leg or worse, do something to someone innocent? The sheer thought of laying aside my pacifist beliefs made me feel sick.

If I didn't comply, would they harm my family? What if it got worse? What if I said no today and tomorrow I wished I had said yes? Maybe this was all a farce because I was innocent, or maybe it wasn't. Could I refuse until I died, or did I risk never seeing my family again, or worse, not being able to ensure their safety?

What if my family was part of this test? What would I do then? My freedom was not worth their safety, but was their safety worth my freedom?

The night stretched on, my mind a turbulent sea of fears and doubts. I tried to rationalize my situation, but every thought looped back to the same terrifying conclusion: I was at their mercy, and the cost of failure was unthinkable. Sleep was impossible. I lay on the cold floor, the hard surface pressing into my bones, and waited for dawn, my thoughts dark and heavy.

As the first light of morning seeped through the cracks of the room, a sense of dread settled over me. I turned the radio back on, listening to the voices. Some were weeping and saying, "What have I done?" while others were dead silent. Did they go through with it? Did they not? Were they allowed to leave? Did they end up like Arnold? I didn't know. All I knew was that my turn was coming.

The speaker turned on and asked me to recite my name and number. My voice trembled as I complied. Then it asked me a series of questions.

"What scares you?"
"What makes you feel uneasy?"

"What are you capable of?"
"What are you not capable of?"
"Why are you here?"

Each question felt like a psychological probe, digging into the deepest corners of my mind. I started to think about my responses when the speaker came back on. "Thank you for participating in the evaluation. Please note that if you choose to follow through with the evaluation task, you will gain your freedom, and all charges will be immediately dropped, and you can proceed with your previous life. A vehicle will escort you to the onboarding facility where you will be discharged. However, if you are unable to fulfill or choose not to participate in the evaluation task, your number will be escalated and all indirect participants, including external parties, may result in compromise. This will result in an escalated, second, evaluation task. You may proceed to door number two."

I walked to door number two, my heart in my throat. I walked over and opened the door. I entered into a small hallway with another door in the distance. As I entered the hallway, the door behind me slammed shut. I tried to jiggle it open, but I couldn't. As I looked further into the hallway, I saw what looked like a small note attached to the door.

I knew it was too late for me to go back, so I went further to investigate, and as I approached the door, the image became more familiar to me. I saw a familiar photo, of a woman and her child playing in the sand at the beach. The sight of their faces was both a comfort and a torment. That photo I have seen several times before, as it previously rested on my nightstand. I snatched the photo off the door and examined it further. On the back it had one word written "REMINDER". I was lost in reality and speechless beyond words. Through the door I could tell there was an awful smell, a mix of rot and decay, but also the sweet scent of honey wafting from the room.

As I stood there, the loudspeaker made one final announcement. "What would you do for the safety of your family?" In a voice only I could hear, I said…

…Anything.

—— End ——